Wendy Helps Out

by Alison Inches
illustrated by Joe and Terri Chicko

Ready-to-Read

Simon Spotlight

New York   London   Toronto   Sydney   Singapore

Based upon the television series *Bob the Builder*™
created by HIT Entertainment PLC and Keith Chapman,
with thanks to HOT Animation, as seen on Nick Jr.®

SIMON SPOTLIGHT
An imprint of Simon & Schuster Children's Publishing Division
1230 Avenue of the Americas, New York, New York 10020

Library of Congress Cataloging-in-Publication Data

Inches, Alison
Wendy helps out / by Alison Inches.-1st ed.
p. cm. - (Bob the builder ; 2)
Summary: When Bob the builder is too sick to work, his assistant
Wendy helps the trucks fix the road for him.
ISBN 0-689-84391-7
[1. Trucks-Fiction. 2. Roads-Maintenance and repair-Fiction.
3. Friendship-Fiction. 4. Sick-Fiction.] I. Title. II. Series.
PZ7.I355 Di 2001
[E]-dc21   2001020177

"Ah-choo!" has a cold.

BOB

"Who will help us fix the ?" asked the machines.

ROAD

"I can!" said .

WENDY

"Hooray!" cheered.
LOFTY

"**Can we *fix it?***"

"**Yes, we can!**"

"I can mix the ,"
CEMENT

said .
DIZZY

"I can spread the ,"
CEMENT

said .
MUCK

"And I can roll it!"

said .
ROLEY

The machines went to
work.  mixed the ⬭.
DIZZY   CEMENT
Then  saw a 🔴.
         DIZZY   BALL

"Look, a !" shouted

BALL

. "Watch me

DIZZY

score!"

kicked

DIZZY

the .

BALL

Splat! "Oops!" said .
DIZZY

"I am stuck in the wet !"
CEMENT

 to the rescue!
LOFTY

"Back to work," said WENDY.

"The 🛣️ must be fixed
ROAD
by 🕛 !"
FIVE O'CLOCK
Mix! Pour! Roll!

"We did it!" said the machines.

WENDY cut the tape at FIVE O'CLOCK.

"Hooray!"

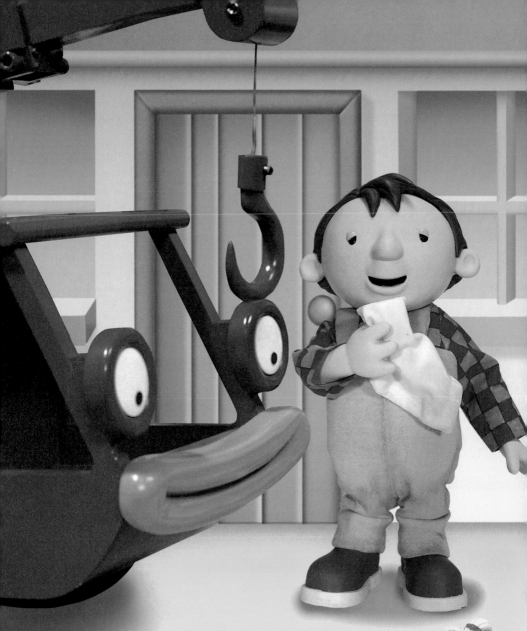

"The 🛣 is fixed," said 👩.
ROAD   WENDY

"Ah-choo! Thanks, 👩,"
WENDY

said 👷.
BOB

"You are welcome,  ,"
BOB

said  .
WENDY

Then it was time for .

BED

"Good night,  ."
BOB

"Good night,  ."
WENDY

"Good night, , , ,

LOFTY   ROLEY   SCOOP

and ."

DIZZY

"Ah-choo!" said .

MUCK